39 Dreams and Stars

39 Dreams and Stars is the first book in the 39 Dreams series telling the tale of the adventures on, in and under Fluffington Moor.

Sue's inspiration to write these books started following the many adventures and fun she had with her stepson and the magical characters that visited them from time to time.

Life should be made of adventures, challenges and happiness. The world is a magical place full of exploration and joy, however sometimes you have to look harder to find it. Keep adventuring and keep challenging yourself to do something new, the future, your future, can be changed. The past is in the past, it should never be forgotten but we should always learn and face our new challenges with a smile and forgiveness.

To Thor

You are the inspiration
Your imagination and enthusiasm for life knows
no bounds
You can achieve anything you want to
All you need to do is believe

Contents

Chapter 1
The Stars

The sun was setting, the sky was getting darker and the trees blew gently in the breeze. The hustle and bustle of the day had gone. The children playing on the climbing frames and the dogs playing ball, had all gone home. All was quiet on Fluffington Moor, or so any normal person would be led to believe.
If you were to walk around Fluffington Moor at sunset you may just be lucky enough to see the faint sparkling stars twinkling near the top of the biggest tree, with the biggest trunk and the highest branches.
You see, high above the ground, way up high in the very top branches of the biggest tree with the biggest trunk was the most secret, hidden location of the SS FATE, the Secret School of Fun, Adventure, Treasure and Excitement.
As the sky got darker the twinkling stars of the SS FATE flashed as they arrived.
Berti was always the first to arrive, she always landed on the north side of the tree. She was strong and clever and always believed that everyone had the power to do anything that they wanted to. They just needed to believe in themselves.
Toby and Terry always arrived together on the South side. Toby and Terry were twins and they were always up to mischief. They were never evil or unkind, but they loved to make everyone

laugh by hiding and pulling pranks on their friends. Toby and Terry loved nothing more than to be adventurous and push everything to the limits.

Gordon arrived on the West side of the tree. He was kind however he was strict and always wanted to play by the rules so the twins had nicknamed him Grumpy.

"I wonder what is behind the door tonight?" asked Berti, whilst switching off her star and opening the door of the headquarters of the SS FATE. Gordon rolled his eyes, he did that a lot, "do we have to take these two with us?" he asked whilst rolling his eyes in the direction of Terry and Toby.

Before Berti could answer, Toby and Terry ran past her and through the door screaming and waving their stars around.

"Turn out your stars" shouted Berti, as Toby and Terry ran up the stairs to the office at the very top of the tree.

"How many times do I have to tell you both?" Shouted Berti.

Toby and Terry laughed and danced about at the top of the stairs waving their stars about and creating pretty light trails in the darkness.

"If we turn them out, we can't see where we are running" they both shouted back at the same time.

Toby and Terry always talked at the same time.

"So do not run and wait until I turn the lights on." Shouted Berti, "you two are so impatient."

There was a loud crash from the top of the stairs and Toby and Terry came tumbling down and landed at Gordon's feet. They lay on the floor

laughing loudly and rolling around. They were laughing so much they could not speak and could not stand up.
Berti stepped over them both and pulled the acorn that hung from the string at the bottom of the stairs to turn on the lights.
A soft glow lit up the wooden staircase that was carved up inside the tree trunk. Gordon closed the door, stepped over Toby and Terry, who were still laughing so much they could not stand up, and followed Berti up the winding wooden staircase to the very top of the tree.
At the top of the staircase, at the very highest point of the biggest tree with the biggest trunk, it opened out onto a large circular platform covered in a massive glass dome. From the inside you could see all across Fluffington Moor for miles and miles. You could see all the way to the flickering streetlights of the big city on one side and all the way to the darkness of the biggest mountain on the Moor, Mount Thunder. Round the outside of the dome ran a platform, so when the moon was bright and the sky was clear, the team could stand out on the platform and feel the wind in their hair and smell the fresh air of the Moor.
Berti pulled another acorn that hung from the ceiling and soft lights lit up the inside of the dome. There was a huge circular desk carved out of the center of the tree with different coloured chairs for each of the team. Berti's was green, Gordons's was orange and Toby and Terry had
yellow, as they both had to have the same. There were three other chairs in purple, red and blue

but they were empty tonight as the others had not arrived.

Finally, Toby and Terry came running into the dome, both red faced and out of breath, but still laughing ridiculously hard.

"Ok, enough now, let us get to work" Berti said "Let us see what we have in the Dream Door tonight."

The Dream Door was the magical door that was carved into the side of the tree, behind which Dreams would arrive each night for the SS FATE team to make come true. The dreams could be from anyone, they could be about anything, but they had a to be a dream that was pure of heart and not a reward for the requestor.

So, you may be wondering how a staircase and a magic door got inside the biggest tree, with the biggest trunk and highest branches on Fluffington Moor. Also, how Berti, Gordon, Toby and Terry knew it was there and what exactly did the SS FATE team do?

Many years ago, when Berti was a teeny, tiny bunny she lived near the lake on Fluffington Moor in a burrow with her mummy and daddy and twelve brothers and sisters. Berti was always the cleverest of the bunnies however she always wanted her brothers and sisters to succeed. Berti helped them with their homework and always made sure that they got to school on time. As the years went by Berti's brothers and sisters moved out and eventually, there was only Berti left in the burrow. Now she had no one left to help, so she went out one evening to find someone that she could help.

As she hopped around the lake, she came to the small wooden bridge that crossed over the narrowest part of the middle of the lake. As she got to the middle of the bridge, she looked over the edge and into the lake. The lake was still, not even a whisper of a breeze, it was like a mirror, but Berti could not see her reflection.

She had stood on this bridge and looked at her reflection many times over the years. Before when the lake was still, she had always seen her reflection, but not on this night, all she saw was the reflection of the moon and the twinkling stars.

As she stared into the lake one star became brighter and brighter and started to move slowly across the sky. Berti watched the star as it flickered brightly in the sky but still it moved slowly further and further away. She leant further over the bridge to see where the star was going. The further Berti leant over the bridge the further away the star would get.

Eventually she leant to far, lost her balance and fell over the side of the bridge and into the lake. Suddenly the bright star flew into the lake and straight to Berti. She grabbed at the star; it was like a cross between a giant icicle and a star. As she grabbed hold of the star it pulled her up to the surface of the lake and across to the edge. Berti scrambled out of the lake, shook herself off and sat down to examine the icicle star.

It was about as long as her hand, had a diamond shape at the top and bottom, had six sides and had the glow of a beautiful white light. Berti could not take her eyes off it, it was so beautiful and smooth. She turned it over in her

hand and as
she turned it the outside felt to get colder and colder like an icicle would.
As she sat there staring at the star, out of the corner of her eye, she saw another star coming slowly towards her. She stood up and watched as the star slowly got closer and closer.
Slowly out of the darkness came a short and rather rotund looking little man.
He had a tall pointy hat and a long white beard. Berti thought he looked like a teeny tiny Santa Claus, but he looked a lot angrier than Santa Claus.
"Did you throw this at me?" shouted the little Santa
Berti started to reply "Errrm No, that wasn't me, I only just…."
But was rudely interrupted by the little Santa
"Well if it wasn't you, who was it? I want to know! I do not appreciate being woken up with an icicle on my head"
"I only just got this one" Berti tried to explain "I fell into the lake and then it just came to me"
The little Santa tilted his head to one side and studied Berti. Suddenly he did not appear so angry. He sat down at the side of the lake and patted the ground next to him. "Tell me everything that happened" he said.
Berti began telling her story "Well I was hopping around the lake, and I hopped onto the bridge. When I got halfway across, I looked over the edge into the lake and the water was so still that I thought I would see my reflection, but I did not."
"What did you see?" Asked the little Santa.

"I saw the reflection of the moon and stars and then one of the stars started glowing brighter and moving. It was moving across the sky; I was trying to see where it was going, I must have leant to far over the bridge as I fell in." she explained

The little Santa interrupted Berti "and let me guess, it all went dark and then the star appeared and pulled you back to the edge of the lake"

"Yes" cried Berti, "How did you know?"

"There is an ancient tale, that I was sure was a fable, well until now at least" explained the little Santa. "The tale says that at midnight on the middle day of the year, when the sky is clear, and the weather is calm a dream will come true. However, the dream has to be true of heart and not a reward for the requestor"

Berti was puzzled, what did this mean and why did this little Santa have an icicle too? Why did he know this tale and she had never heard it before? There were so many questions running through her head.

"What were you thinking about as you looked at
the moon and stars?" asked the little Santa.

Berti looked up to the sky and across to the moon and tried to remember what she was thinking about. She remembered looking up at the stars and all the times she had sat by the lake with her brothers and sisters picking out the different constellations and giving them funny names, she gave them funny names to make her brothers and sisters laugh. She was

remembering all the things she did to help them and make sure that they were always happy then it all went dark as she tumbled into the lake.
She looked across at the little Santa and explained that she was thinking about her family, making them happy and wishing that she could do it again.
"So, you were dreaming of making others happy?" Asked little Santa
"Yes, I suppose I was" Berti replied.
"Well, that sounds like a dream that is true of heart and not a reward to me" said little Santa and as he said this, two more stars came flying towards them at great speed.
Flying behind the two stars were two screaming and laughing, blue and red clad pixies. They came to a sudden stop in front of Berti and little Santa.
Suddenly all four stars pulled their new owners together to form one big shining giant star. There was a flash and colouredA stars started flying around them. Then in a blink of an eye all four of them were stood on a platform, by a large glass dome, way up in the sky.
They all sat down immediately and looked about.
"Where are we?" asked Berti "What just happened?"
Little Santa looked at the other three and said "So it's true"
"What's true?" Asked the two little red and blue pixies at the same time.
Little Santa looked out across the moor and

then slowly turned back and quietly said “The tale of the SS FATE”
For a moment there was silence and then came a voice from behind them “It is no tale, it is true” the voice said.

Chapter 2
The Inspector

The tail of the SS FATE was a story that had been told on Fluffington Moor for many years, but no one knew if it was true. It was a tale that parents told to children at bedtime or when they were out on a picnic on Fluffington Moor. Everyone loved a good tale, but maybe this tale was more of a truth.

The Tail of The SS FATE

It is said that at midnight on the middle day of the year, in the middle of Fluffington Moor, in the middle of the bridge, that crosses the middle of the lake. When the sky is clear and the weather is calm, if someone looks into the lake, a dream will come true. The dream has to be true of heart and not a reward for the requestor. It has to be kind and thoughtful, loving and caring.
It is said that those that look into the lake at midnight, on the middle day of the year, from the middle of the bridge, in the middle of Fluffington Moor, will see the moon and the stars but they will not see their reflection.
If they cannot see their reflection, in the calm waters of the lake, it is because they are true of heart, they are kind and they are thoughtful and they do not need their reflection to know this.

Those that see their reflection will see it because they need to. They need to see themselves to know they are there. Those that do not see their reflection

care for others more than themselves. They want to see what is around them and not themselves.
It is said that if this person has a dream that will help others and not themselves, they will receive the Star of KiKo. A star from far, far away, which is locked in diamonds and glows so brightly it can be seen for miles around.
It is said that if you possess The Star of KiKo you would never get older and you will live forever. The Star of KiKo would only disappear if you are no longer true of heart.
It is said that the Star of KiKo will create starlets called Tigers, which will go to those that need help. Those that need fun, excitement and Adventure.
It is said that many, many years ago there was a woman, no one knew her name, they just called her The Inspector. She had a Star of KiKo and it took her to the top of the biggest tree, with the biggest trunk and the highest branches where she could see all across Fluffington Moor and to far beyond.
It is said that The Inspector made a home in the biggest tree, with the biggest trunk and the highest branches. In the tree she carved a door where each night there would be a dream. She would then look out across the land for the Tiger Starlet, the brightest shining light around, and she would know that is who she needed to help.

For many years, The Inspector had made dreams come true from her home high up in the biggest tree, with the biggest trunk and the highest branches on Fluffington Moor.

When The Inspector made dreams come true it was not like in the films, you could not just think of something and it happened, O no, not with The Inspector. A dream granted by The Inspector had to be worked for, it had to be appreciated. It had to be understood that dreams were not magic, dreams could always come true if you worked hard enough to achieve them. So, with The Inspector, it was like a secret school. You never knew you were learning, but eventually the outcome would be either Fun, Adventure, Treasure or excitement, or maybe even all four. She had called her home the SS FATE, which she said, stood for the Secret School of Fun, Adventure, Treasure and Excitement as that was what she believed the dreams she granted gave everyone.

The Inspector had always been alone in the SS FATE as no one else had ever looked into the lake on the middle day of the year, at midnight and not seen their reflection. She had always dreamt, rather selfishly, that she had some help. You see there were so many dreams, and she could only do one at a time, so she believed she was letting down all those with dreams that she could not grant and this made her sad. She granted as many dreams as she could, but her dream of help never seemed to come true. When The Inspector had made her home in the biggest tree, with the biggest trunk and the highest branches, she had made room for others to join her. At the very top of the tree there was the large circular platform which was mostly covered by a large hexagonal clear glass dome where The Inspector could sit and look for the Starlets. Underneath she had built bedrooms and a lovely comfortable sitting room to rest in, she had even made chairs in the dome and had carefully painted them different colours, hers was red, as red was her favourite colour. The chairs all spun round and The Inspector loved to sit in her chair and spin round so that she could see right across the moor and keep an eye on what was going on.

One night, The Inspector was sat in her chair planning for the next dream when suddenly, shortly after midnight, on the middle day of the year, on the platform outside the dome, in the biggest tree with the biggest trunk and the highest branches, she saw four shadows.

No one had ever been on her platform before, no one knew how to get up to it. The platform could only be seen by those that possessed a Star of KiKo. Those that were true of heart and wanted to help others without reward. Could it be true, could they have Stars of KiKo, could they be here to help her.

She quietly got up from her chair and crept to the door. She quietly opened it, just a crack, so she could hear what they were saying.

She heard a female voice ask, "Where are we? what just happened?" And then a male voice said "So it's true"

"What's true?" Asked the other two at the same time.

The male voice replied "The tale of the SS FATE"

The Inspector quietly opened the door a little wider and quietly walked out "It is no tale, it is true" she said to them.

The four shadows turned towards the voice and the Inspector's heart jumped with joy. They were all holding Stars of KiKo, they had come to help her, she was so excited. She finally, after all these years, had help. They would be able to grant so many dreams. There were two small pixies', a Jarlie, which was a cross between an elf and a troll, and a rabbit. she was just so happy that she did not realise that she was just stood there staring at them.

"I cannot believe it's true" said the Jarlie "I just cannot believe it. I have lived here for many years but I never thought it was true. I have never seen this platform or dome before. I just do not understand"

The Inspector stood back and looked at each of them "You could not see it because you did not have the Star. Now you have the Star of KiKo you have the power to live forever and grant the dreams of those wish them."

"But I don't understand" said the Jarlie, "the tale says that only those that look into the lake at midnight and do not see their reflection would get a Star of KiKo. I have not looked in the lake, I was asleep in my mound"

The Inspector looked out towards the lake and thought for a moment. Was it really her dream coming true, was her dream true of heart? She thought so, as she only wanted help grant dreams for others, but was it a reward. She supposed it was a reward, of sorts, but as well as being a reward for herself it would reward everyone that she granted dreams for. So yes, after all these years of being on her own she believed her dream had come true.

"You are correct," she said, "only those that look into the lake, with a true heart and not seeking reward will receive the Star of KiKo." The Inspector paused and looked again at all their faces. They all looked truly shocked. "I have long been dreaming of help" she said, "and so I can only assume that my dream has come true, and this is why you have also received a Star of KiKo. Come, come inside I must know more about you" and with that The Inspector led them all into the dome. She made them all hot chocolate with cream and marshmallows, as it was cold out on the platform, and they each chose a chair to sit in.

"So, tell me your names first" said the Inspector, "my name is Sue, but, if you have heard the tale, you will know me as The Inspector."

"My name is Berti, and I live in a burrow by the lake," said the rabbit

"My name is Gordon," said the jarlie "and I live in the mossy mound by the playground."

"Our names are Toby and Terry" said the pixies "and we live in the cherry tree by the big house"

"This is so exciting" said Inspector Sue. "So long I have dreamt of help and here you all are, we will have so much fun, I can't wait to get started"

Suddenly the SS FATE started to shake, the whole tree was shaking, in fact the whole of Fluffington Moor was shaking. Everyone hung on tight their chairs and looked out of the dome across the moor.

"What is happening?" cried Berti as she hung on as tightly as she could to her chair.

"Hold on tight" said Inspector Sue.

Chapter 3
The Protector

Right on the edge, on the farthest point, in the darkest corner of Fluffington Moor was the tallest mountain with the highest peaks. Peaks so high that sometimes they would disappear above the clouds and be covered in deep, fluffy snow.
Deep inside the mountain hid a secret, a secret that was not known to anyone, this was a secret that had been hidden for many, many years.
The Mountain was known, to everyone on Fluffington Moor, as Thunder Mountain as every now and again the Mountain would emit loud sounds that sounded like thunder. No one knew where the noise came from, only that it came from deep inside the Mountain and could be heard all across Fluffington Moor.
Many times, people had tried to climb the mountain. They had tried to find a way inside to try and find where the sound was coming from but each time they had failed. No one could find the entrance, no one could find a way into the heart of the Mountain.
Many years before, unknown to Inspector Sue, someone else had looked into the lake from the middle of the bridge, at midnight on the middle day of the year. Someone else had been granted a Star, but it was not a Star of KiKo, it was a Star of Thunder. Someone else had been granted eternal life, but the Star of Thunder was granted

to someone that would be a protector, someone that would guard and look after those that could not look after themselves. However, they had not been sent to the SS FATE. They had been sent into the Mountain.

That someone had landed in the middle of a bridge, over a trickling stream, in a beautiful cavern, right in the middle of the Mountain. The ceiling and walls sparkled with blue/green crystals and the floor was covered in deep, soft green moss. Small shafts of light came from the walls, bounced off the crystals and lit up the whole cavern. It was breath taking.
This was where the secret was kept, the secret was not the beautiful cavern with the waterfall and crystal walls, but a whole other secret that had been buried many years before.
It was to this cavern, in the middle of the mountain, that TJ had landed at midnight, on the middle day of the year all those years ago.
In his hand he held the Star of Thunder, a beautiful hexagonal crystal with different colours on each side. He turned it over in his hands and thought how unusual it was, but right now he was more interested in where he was than the crystal. He popped the crystal in his jacket pocket to keep it safe.
"Hello" TJ shouted, but all he heard was the sound of the waterfall tumbling down into the stream.
"Hellooooooooo, anyone here?" He shouted
again, still all he heard was the sound of the waterfall tumbling into the stream.

TJ looked around and was utterly amazed by the wonderful cavern that surrounded him. He wasn't sure how he had got here and wasn't sure how he would get out, but that was a worry for later. The cavern was beautiful with crystals glistening from the walls and the peaceful sound of the stream running through it.
As he walked off the bridge and onto the mossy floor it was bouncy like a trampoline. He jumped and the moss was so bouncy he flew high up in the cavern. This was so much fun, he laughed and slowly floated down again. It was like he could fly. He jumped again and went higher and higher towards the roof of the cavern, it was such fun.
As he was bouncing around, he saw that high up in the roof of the cavern was a ledge, like a shelf in the top of the cavern. It was certainly big enough for him to get onto, but he just had to get there. He bounced even higher and twisted left and right to try and get closer. With one final bounce he flew high up into the top of the cavern and onto the ledge.
TJ scrambled onto the ledge; he could see all across the cavern. He was certainly high up, but he was not scared, in fact he was having too much fun to be scared.
As he looked more closely at the walls, he saw that it was not shafts of light that lit up the cavern it was tiny little people, like tiny fairies, but they were glowing. They were glowing brightly like little stars.
"Hello" TJ said quietly to one of the tiny little fairy people but all he heard was a squeak.

"I don't understand you" he said, again all he heard was a little squeak.
The tiny fairy person was pointing to his jacket pocket. He put his hand to his pocket and felt the crystal that he had earlier, he had almost forgotten all about it.
TJ took the Star of Thunder from his pocket and turned it in his hands. As he turned it, he noticed it was two pieces that appeared to be fastened together. He tried to pull them apart, but they would not move. He tried pushing them together, but they still would not move. He then tried twisting it and it moved. Just like one of those cubes with lots of coloured stickers on. With each turn of the hexagonal sides there was a click and the star glowed brightly from one of the coloured sides. First green, then blue, then purple, then, just as it turned yellow there was a loud bang. A bang so loud that it shook the mountain and almost shook TJ off the ledge. He grabbed at the wall but dropped the star. The whole mountain was shaking.
"You need to turn it again to stop the shaking" shouted a voice from above TJs head. "Quick grab it and turn it to red, come on quickly,"
TJ reached for the star, but it was getting dangerously close to the edge of the ledge. He made a quick lunge for it and managed to grab it just before it fell off and down into the stream below.
He scrambled back to the safety of the wall and quickly turned it again and it glowed bright red. As suddenly as it started, the shaking stopped and the cavern fell quiet again. All he could hear

was the waterfall and beating of his own heart. He looked up to where the voice had come from and the tiny fairy person that had been sat there was now gone. The tiny hole in the wall was empty and the glow of the light had gone.

"Where did you go? Are you still here?" TJ cried

"Please tell me your still here"

After a couple of seconds, the tiny fairy person reappeared in the hole.

"You really need to learn how to use that thing you know; you can't just go about twisting it to your hearts content and watching all the pretty colours" she said

"Hang on a minute" TJ said "if you had explained that to me when I spoke to you before instead of just squeaking at me then maybe it would not have happened"

The tiny fairy ignored TJ's comment, "Do you even know what you are holding in your hand?" She asked

"I have no idea," said TJ "One minute I was stood in the middle of the bridge, in the middle of the lake on Fluffington Moor and the next I am stood on that bridge down there holding this. Where am I and what is this thing?" He asked

"You really don't know do you?" The tiny fairy person said, "You really don't know the power that you now have do you?"

TJ was starting to get annoyed with this little person "Do you really think I would be asking and making mountains shake whilst I am sat on a ledge a million miles over a running stream in a cavern, in the middle of a mountain if I knew?" he

said angrily
"Ok, no need to get annoyed," the tiny fairy person said "let's start from the beginning shall we. My name is Shelby, and I am a Farlight. Farlights only exist here, and we are the guardians of the Cavern and its hidden secrets. We have been waiting for a long time for someone to come with the Star of Thunder to help free us"
TJ had never heard of the hidden secrets of the Mountain and had certainly never heard of the Farlights that were the guardians of it. His anger had subsided and now he was intrigued to know more.
Shelby continued, "What you have in your hand is the Star of Thunder."
"The Star of Thunder?" TJ questioned; he had never heard of this either.
"The Star of Thunder is granted to someone that has the heart of a protector" Shelby explained "the Star has special powers depending on the colour that it is on"
"Special powers?" Asked TJ. What could this mean, what would he be able to do now? Could he grant wishes? This was extremely exciting.
"So, each colour of each side does different things" explained Shelby. "Green lets you fly, Blue lets you swim deep underwater, Purple lets you climb, Yellow, well Yellow you know. Yellow makes the Mountain shake and as it shakes it makes sounds like Thunder."
Shelby paused as TJ was staring at her in disbelief.
"Are you telling me that I can fly, I can swim under water without oxygen and I can climb up

anything I want to?" He asked
"Yes" she replied, "however the star will only work outside of the cavern if you are using its powers to protect something or someone"
"What do the other colours do?" asked TJ, excited to know what else he was able to do
"Red stops the mountain shaking" Shelby said "and finally black, black returns you to being you. The you that arrived here tonight. That is the safest colour to have the star on when you are not using it"
This was a lot to take in for TJ. He had so many questions. Why would he need to fly or swim without oxygen or climb up things and why would he need to make a Mountain shake? Just so many questions, it was too much to take in.
"I think I need to get down from here" TJ said, thinking that getting his feet back on solid ground may help him work all this out.
"You need to turn the star two turns to the right onto Green" Shelby told him "Then you just need to step off the ledge, relax and you will float to the ground"
"Are you insane?" Cried out TJ. "You want me to twist this thing two turns and then just step off? I will fall to my death"
"You need to trust me" whispered Shelby "You need to trust the Star. Two turns and step off, off you go"
TJ really was not sure about this, in fact at this point he was quite sure he was dreaming.
He turned the star over in his hands and then very slowly turned it once. Just as Shelby had said it turned black.

"It worked" he exclaimed "it went black like you said" but all he heard from Shelby was squeaking. He looked across at her and she squealed louder at him. He picked her up and dropped her into his top pocket. "If I'm going over this edge, so are you" he told her.
He turned the star one more twist to the right and sure enough it turned green.
TJ suddenly felt lighter. He did a little jump and went so high that he bumped his head on the ceiling.
"Relax" Shelby shouted from his pocket, "You have done this before, it is just like you were jumping before but in reverse."
"That easy for you to say" TJ replied
He tried to relax and slowly he floated back to the shelf
He looked down into his pocket "Hang on, you're not squeaking again" he said.
"You can only hear me when you are not on Black. When you are on black you have no powers, so you do not have the power to hear me." Shelby told him
"Well, that makes about as much sense as everything else you have told me so far." TJ scolded her. "Ok hang on tight"
With a tight grip on the star and a protective hand over Shelby in his pocket, TJ took another jump up from the ledge. As he got towards the roof he relaxed and bent away from ledge. Slowly, just as before, he started to descend back down to the cavern floor.
As his feet touched the floor he sat down on the deep, soft moss. This was so much to take in.

"I told you so" said Shelby
TJ looked at her yawned and laughed. "You certainly did," he said, his eyes lit up "let's go swim under water, come on you have to take me now."
Shelby looked at him, one eye brow raised, was flying not enough for this guy. She guessed not as he was sat looking at her with pleading eyes.
"Oh, please, come on, surely I get to try out the swimming now that I have mastered flying." Said TJ
Shelby sighed, "You have done so much today," she said, "I think a nap would be good and we can try swimming tomorrow"
"I am tired" said TJ, "maybe just a little nap and then we go swimming" he yawned and laughed again. With that he stretched out on the soft moss and fell straight to sleep.

Chapter 4
The Farlights

Some hours later TJ woke up, he stretched and lay still with his eyes closed remembering his dream.
It was so much fun and he had been able to fly. The cavern that he had been in was just so beautiful and there were little glowing fairy lights. Not forgetting, of course, the Star of Thunder, which had impressive powers.
He wished that he had been able to have a go at swimming underwater, he wanted to know how he would breathe, but it was just a dream, a wonderful, wonderful dream.
He stretched again; he was just so comfortable.
"Are you awake?" Came a voice over his head. "Come on, you've been asleep for hours,"
TJ slowly opened his eyes; the light was so bright and there was a buzzing over his head. He sat up and the light moved and then he realised that his dream was not a dream, it was real. He was still in the cavern sat on the soft mossy floor.
"Finally! Your awake" came a voice from the flying light.
TJ looked at the light, "Shelby? Is that you?" He asked
"Of course, it's me, who did you think it was?" She said.
"So, this is real? I really have a Star of Thunder? I can really swim under water" TJ exclaimed excitedly.

Shelby landed on the moss in front of him and immediately vanished up to her neck. She was so tiny and the moss was so deep "Yes of course it's real." She said, "were you not paying attention last night?"
TJ looked at the little Farlight, he still could not believe that he was here. Even more, he could not believe that he now had magic powers.
"Let's be honest" he said, "If you were out for a walk and then suddenly you ended up in a cavern being told you had the powers to fly, swim underwater and climb up anything, would you think it was real?"
Shelby climbed up onto TJ's leg and looked up at him. "I suppose you are right" she said, "it is a lot to take in, but come on, I have lots to show you and you have lots of Farlights to meet"
As Shelby said this all the other shining lights from the walls flew down towards her. There was now a bright ball of light in front of TJ.
"These are the rest of the Farlights." She explained "This is Shaun, Simon, Shelia, Stella, Sandra, Simone, Stephanie, Suzi and Stevie"
TJ interrupted her, "Hold it right there" he said, "Are you telling me that all the Farlights names start with S?"
Shelby looked across the Farlights and then back to TJ "Why yes" she said, "All our names start with S as we are all Special, that is except Victor and Vicky, they are the Grand Rulers of the Farlights"
Now TJ was even more confused, "You have Grand Rulers" he asked

As he said this the crowd of Farlights parted and through the middle appeared a faint blue light. As the blue light got closer TJ realised that it was two more Farlights, a man and a woman. They were older, had long cloaks and crowns and had blue lights instead of the bright sunshine yellow of the other Farlights.
Shelby bowed down low as the two blue Farlights approached TJ.
"Who are they?" Asked TJ
"Shushhhhhhh, wait for them to speak" whispered Shelby
The male Farlight stepped forward and up onto TJ's knee, "So you are the Great One," he said, "you are the one chosen to free us from the cavern. My name is Victor Farlight and this is my wife, Vicky Farlight we are the Grand Rulers of the Farlights"
TJ pinched himself, just to make sure he really wasn't dreaming. This was getting crazier by the minute. Not only did he have magic powers but now he was the Great One. He was to free the Farlights but free them from what. There were so many questions that now TJ had forgotten what the first ones were.
TJ looked at Victor and across to Vicky and back again. He wanted to ask so many questions but which one to ask first.
Victor took a step forward on TJ's knee "You want to know why you are here don't you?" he said
"I think that would help" TJ said, "If I knew why I was here maybe I could start to understand what is going on."
All the Farlights sat down on the moss and

suddenly, the cavern went darker. All the Farlights apart from Shelby, Victor and Vicky had disappeared into the deep moss when they sat down.
Victor sat down on TJ's knee and cleared his throat. "I will start at the beginning" he said, "it's always a good place to start."
As he started to speak all the other Farlights flew up from the moss and back to their holes in the walls ready to listen to the story.
Victor continued, "Many years ago a dragon lived in the mountain and he would steal treasure from the villagers of Fluffington. He would bring the treasure back to the cavern and hide it away so that they would never find it. The villagers feared the dragon and they wanted it to leave. One night, when the villagers had finally had enough of the dragon, they found the biggest piece of treasure that the dragon had not taken and they filled it with dynamite. When the Dragon took the treasure back to his cavern, they exploded the dynamite." Victor paused at this point and looked around the cavern.
"What happened next?" asked TJ
Victor looked at Vicky and then back to TJ "What happened next changed Fluffington forever" he said, "When the dynamite exploded it shook the whole of Fluffington and there was a loud roar as the dragon broke out of the top of the mountain and flew off into the night. The dragon was gone, but the fire that took the mountain was huge. It was blazing from the middle of the mountain and the villagers were scared it would burn down the whole of their village. They started a chain of

buckets to try and get the fire under control, but the fire was just too big. The more water they poured onto the fire the more sparks it shot out into the sky. The fire had never got to the village but many of the villagers were killed trying to put the fire out. Eventually, after eight days the fire burnt itself out and the treasure was lost forever or so the villagers thought." Victor stopped again and sighed loudly.

TJ was staring at Victor, totally enthralled by the story, "What happened to the treasure?" He asked

"That is the secret that only we know" Victor said, "You see the treasure was deep in the middle of mountain and was right next to the dynamite when it went off. As the dynamite blew, the gold all melted together but it got so hot that it started to spark. Each little spark flew high up into the cavern and melted into the wall. As the cavern eventually cooled the sparks created Farlights and we have been trapped inside this cavern ever since." He paused again and looked around the walls at all the Farlights. They were all sat on the edges of their holes. They had heard this story many times, but for some reason this time it was different.

Victor continued his story, "as the cavern started to recover from the fire, the waterfall started to run and it washed away the ash from the fire and as the water ran it revealed two hexagonal crystals with a star trapped in the centre of each. One was bright white, and one was striped, green, blue, purple, yellow, red and black. Many of us tried to pick up the crystals but we could not keep hold of them until the kindest and purest of our

Farlights, tried and he could pick up the white one and the bravest and strongest Farlights picked up the striped one. As they picked them up, there was a flash from the white one and a loud noise, like thunder, from the striped one. Then both the Farlights and the crystal stars vanished and we have not seen them since, well until tonight that is."

The whole cavern was silent, except the trickling of the stream and the rushing waterfall. Everyone was totally enthralled by the story of the dragon and the crystals.

"So, this is called the Star of Thunder because of the noise and the trapped star?" Asked TJ

"That is correct." Said Victor, "The striped one sounded like Thunder so we called it the Star of Thunder and as it could only be touched by the strongest and bravest Farlight we believe that the Star of Thunder will only go to someone that is a protector. As for the other crystal, the word for white, in Farlish, our language, is KiKo so we called the white one the Star of KiKo and as it could only be touched by the kindest and purest of our Farlights we believe that the Star of KiKo will only go to those that are true of heart." Victor paused again.

Things were starting to make sense for TJ now, at least he knew where the name Star of Thunder came from, but now there was a Star of KiKo as well.

Victor continued "We believe that when the Star of Thunder and the Star of KiKo are put back together then we will be free and able to leave the cavern"

But this did not explain where the rest of the treasure was. Was it still in the cavern? Was it TJ's now?
"You are thinking about the treasure aren't you" Victor asked him
TJ looked at Victor with amazement. How did he know? How did he know what he was thinking? "Well, yes, but how did you know that? How did you know what I was thinking?" He asked
Victor looked around again, he looked around a lot, "We can read your mind, I know you are confused and have lots of questions, but it will all become clear eventually. Let us start with the stars, the Star of KiKo is made of all the diamonds from the treasure and in the middle holds a star. The Star of Thunder is made of all the Emeralds, Rubies, Sapphires, Topaz, Amethysts and ash from the fire and it also has a star in the middle. All the gold melted and if you dive to the bottom of the pool under the waterfall you will find three giant disks of gold." Victor explained
TJ was starting to understand now, he knew where the star came from and what it did. He knew where the treasure was, but he still did not know what he had to do.
"You want to know what you need to do don't you?" Victor asked him
TJ started to wonder if there was any point to him talking anymore if he could read his mind, was there really any point?
"Of course, you need to talk TJ," Victor said, "Just because we can read your mind doesn't mean we don't want to talk to you"
TJ looked him straight in the eyes and said, "So

what am I thinking now?" He asked
Victor laughed and blinked his eyes, "I'll do better than tell you, I'll get it for you" and with that Victor blinked twice again and clapped his hands. Immediately a giant cheese and tomato pizza appeared in front of TJ with the biggest chocolate milkshake he had ever seen. Now this, was something TJ could get used to.

Chapter 5
The Thunder

As the biggest tree, with the biggest trunk and the highest branches on Fluffington Moor continued to shake, everyone hung on tightly to their chairs. Inspector Sue looked quite relaxed however Berti, Gordan and the twins, Terry and Toby, looked scared.
Blue sparks continued to fly out of the top of the mountain. Then, as suddenly as it started, it stopped and the mountain returned to being a normal, quiet mountain.
"What on earth was that" cried Berti "I have felt the moor shake before but not like that and I have never seen the blue sparks before" she said.
Inspector Sue looked at the mountain again and then turned back to the others.
She let out a sigh "It is said that when the Star of KiKo was created there was a second Star, the Star of Thunder" she explained, "The Star of Thunder is trapped in the mountain with the Great One. The shaking and the noise is the Star and the Great One trying to get out"
"You mean the stars are twins like us?" Terry and Toby shouted.
Inspector Sue spun round to look at the twins, "Do you have to shout all the time?" she exclaimed.
The twins looked at each other and smirked, they did like to be loud and silly, however maybe now was not the right time.

"However, to answer your question, yes" said Inspector Sue, "The stars are twins like you are, they were both created at the same time. You see a long time ago there was a dragon that lived in the mountain. The villagers of Fluffington wanted the dragon to leave, so the blew it up with dynamite. The explosion caused a huge fire in the mountain. During the fire all the treasure that the dragon had stollen from the village melted and from the ashes came two hexagonal shaped crystals. Each crystal contained a star trapped in the middle of it. One crystal was white and one was multicoloured. The white one was the original Star of KiKo and the multicoloured one, the Star of Thunder." She paused; she knew this was a lot to take in. "Does anyone want more hot chocolate or biscuits" she asked

The twins immediately shot their hands up, "Yes please" they shouted

"Berti? Gordan? Do you want anything?" Inspector Sue asked

"I'd like some sleep" grumbled Gordan, "but I suppose a few biscuits and another hot chocolate would be nice"

"Yes please" replied Berti

Whilst Inspector Sue went off to the kitchen downstairs the others got down from their chairs and looked out of the dome.

They could see for miles and miles.

"I can see my burrow from here" said Berti

"We can see our Cherry Tree," said the twins

"I want to see the back of my eyelids" grumbled Gordan

Inspector Sue returned with the biscuits and hot

chocolate. “Shall I continue the story?” she asked
“Yes please” said Berti as they all returned to their chairs and got ready to listen.
Inspector Sue jumped up onto her chair, “I received the Star of KiKo and, it is said, The Great One, received the Star of Thunder. The Great One lives in the Mountain with the Star of Thunder, like I live here with the Star of KiKo. When the mountain shakes it emits loud sounds like Thunder, that’s why it is called Thunder Mountain. I do not know why the mountain shakes, I would love to help him and understand why, but I only know The Great One exists because the Star of KiKo has shown me a vision of a beautiful cavern inside the mountain with a young man holding the Star of Thunder.”
Inspector Sue paused to take a drink.
“If the Star of KiKo gives is powers to grant dreams, what does the Star of Thunder do” asked Berti
“It is said,” said Inspector Sue, “that the Star of Thunder is given to someone strong and brave that can protect and guide others to protect themselves. From what I understand, the Star of Thunder works the same as the Star of KiKo. The Star of Thunder protects someone or something, however they do not know that it is the star protecting them. The star will guide them into understanding how to protect themselves.”
Suddenly, the tree began to shake again only this time it was shaking even more, and the sound of thunder was louder than it had ever been before. Everyone grabbed onto their chairs, but Gordan could not hold on and fell out of his chair onto the

floor and rolled across the dome. Terry and Toby were scared and held on tightly to each other.
The tree had never shaken like this before. Pictures were falling off the walls, their mugs of hot chocolate flew off the table and there were biscuits scattered everywhere.
Inspector Sue was scared that the shaking would topple the tree, they had to get out of here.
"Quick, everyone hold up your star, we need to touch them together" she shouted over the sound of Thunder and crashing furniture.
Gordan struggled to stand up and get back across the dome to the rest of the team, but he eventually made it.
As everyone held up their stars, they all looked at each other with fear in their eyes.
"On three, everyone put their stars in the middle to touch" shouted Inspector Sue, "One, Two, THREE" she yelled.
As everyone held onto something to stop them falling, they all leant forward and raised their stars together into a point.
As the stars touched, the brightest white light they had ever seen beamed out of the top. It was so bright they all had to close their eyes.
They grabbed to hold someone else's hand as the sound of thunder got louder and the shaking got faster and faster.
Suddenly they were all spinning round and round, faster and faster like they were free falling out of a plane, but instead of going down they were going upwards.
They smashed through the roof of the dome and shot up skywards.

Terry and Toby were screaming. They were spinning so fast now none of them could open their eyes, they could hardly breathe they were going that fast.
Suddenly, they were falling, they were spinning and falling. Falling so fast they still could not open their eyes. Then, as quickly as the shaking of the tree had started, they landed gently, face down, on the softest surface.
They all lay there, not daring move or open their eyes. The shaking and spinning had stopped. The noise had gone and everything around them was quiet.
"Everyone ok" asked Inspector Sue
"I think so" said Berti
"Us too" said Terry and Toby
"Am I still alive?" asked Gordan
Slowly they turned over and opened their eyes and they could not believe what they were seeing.

Chapter 6
The Cavern

"Are we where I think we are?" asked Berti
Inspector Sue looked around, blinked her eyes and blinked them again. She looked back to the group. "I think we are" she replied.
They all sat up and looked around them. They were in a cavern. The cavern, in the middle of the mountain from the story of the Star of Thunder. There was a stream and a waterfall and all the walls glistened with blue/green gems. There were tiny lights all around the walls and they were sat on the softest, deepest mat of moss. All they could hear was the water falling from the waterfall into the stream.
They were on their own, there was no one else here. Where was TJ? Did he really exist or was he just a name in a tale?
"Hello" shouted Inspector Sue, "Is there anyone here?" her voice echoed around the cavern, but they heard nothing but Inspector Sue's voice echoing back to them.
"He must be here; he simply must be. If the Great One is not here, how did the mountain start shaking?" said Inspector Sue. Maybe the story is not true, maybe the vision from her star was just a vision she thought.
"It's not a big cavern, but there looks to be a lot of little caves. Let's split up and search it" suggested Berti.
"Good plan" said Inspector Sue

"If you think I'm moving after all that you can forget it" growled Gordon, "I was woken from my nap with this thing hitting me on the head, I was transported to a tree, I have been shaken off a chair and then spun and dropped in a cave. I feel like I have been through a washing machine on a cold spin wash. I will be staying right here and having a nap. When you have worked out how you are getting me back to my mound, wake me up. Until then, do not disturb me." He said and with that Gordon lay back down and went to sleep.

"Wow, someone's grumpy" said the twins, "Grumpy Gordon" they whispered and giggled.

"Looks like it's just the four of us then" said Bertie, "Terry and Toby, you go across the bridge and search that side of the river and Inspector Sue and I will do this side. Let's go." She said encouragingly.

They split up and began searching, but to be honest there was not much to search. There was the bridge, the stream and mounds and mounds of deep, soft moss with some large rocks here and there. There were some caves off the cavern, but they were all empty and within five minutes they were all back together.

"Shusshhh" said Berti, "what's that noise?" She asked

Toby and Terry started giggling and they all looked across the moss towards Gordon. The noise that Berti could hear was Gordon snoring.

Everyone started to giggle, this was just too much to take in. They had no idea where they were, they had all been on a cold spin cycle and, if they were honest, they were all as tired as Gordon. They did

not want to sleep, their heads were spinning with questions, the main one being, how to get out? They all lay down and stared up at the ceiling of the cavern.
Suddenly Inspector Sue sat up again, "I was thinking" she started to say as Toby and Terry interrupted her, "last time you *'thought'* it got us here, do you really think that you *'thinking'* right now is a clever idea?" They asked and giggled.
"That's my point" said Inspector Sue, "if putting the stars together got us here, maybe putting them together will get us out of here."
Berti, Terry and Toby looked at her, maybe she had a point. What did they have to lose? They had no other ideas and if the stars had got them here, then maybe they could get them out of here.
"Let's be honest," said Berti, "What is the worst that can happen? At the very least we will still be here and at the best it could get us out of here."
Terry and Toby looked at each other, "What have we got to lose?" They asked, "but there is no way that we are waking Grumpy over there up." The twins had decided to call Gordon, Grumpy, maybe not to his face, but certainly whilst he was asleep. "He was grumpy before; can you even imagine how grumpy he will be if we wake him up again?" they said.
"Maybe we don't have to wake him up" said Inspector Sue, "he still has his star in his hand. If we can all get around him without waking him, we can put our stars on his."
Berti did not look convinced "I am not sure that we should" she said
"Come on, what else can we do?" said Inspector

Sue. "We could have a nap and wait until we are all awake and then do it, but do you really think that he will be any less grumpy after a nap. I do not think so."
The twins smiled "let's just do it, at the very least, if we do wake him, he may be so mad that he may just explode and then we can walk out of the hole he makes with his explosion." They both laughed.
"So, we have two options" said Inspector Sue, "number one, let's all take a nap and wait for Gordon to wake up, but he may still be grumpy and may not want to go through another 'cold spin cycle' or number two, take a chance and all put our stars to his whilst he is asleep. Yes, we risk falling on him or waking him and maybe nothing happening but, if we manage to touch all the stars and it gets us back to the SS FATE it will make him happy. I am in favour of number two, who is with me?"
"I'm in" said Berti
The twins looked at each other and then back to Inspector Sue, "Let's do it, number two it is, but if he wakes up grumpier than he was when he went to sleep, we are going to deny all responsibility of any involvement what's so ever." They said.
"Ok, Ok, if he gets grumpier, I will take all the responsibility" said Inspector Sue, "So let's do this. Let us all take different sides of him. I will take the position furthest away as I have the longest arms, then you Berti and then you guys" she said, looking at the twins, "you need to be the closest as you have the smallest arms"
The twins really were not sure about this. If they

were the closest then, if he woke up, they would be in the direct firing line of a severely grumpy Gordon.

"Do we really need to be that close to him?" They asked

"It's not our fault you both have the shortest arms" Inspector Sue told them

"Pull yourselves together.," said Berti, "come on, we have to do this or we will be stuck here forever. Do you really want to be stuck in this cavern with no food or drinks and even more to the point, with a very grumpy Gordon?" Asked Berti

"You make a very good point" replied the twins. "Ok let's do this."

They all stood up as quietly as they could so as not to wake Gordon and slowly moved into their positions.

"On three" whispered Inspector Sue, "One, Two, Three"

They all moved their stars towards Gordon's and held their breath as they touched them all together.

As the stars touched the bright white light reappeared. They all closed their eyes and dreamt of their homes on Fluffington Moor. Inspector Sue dreamt of the headquarters, Berti of her burrow by the lake and the twins of their cherry tree by the big house.

The air around them got colder. It kept getting colder and colder. They all kept their eyes shut, held each other's hands tightly and did not say a word so they would not wake Gordon.

Chapter 7
The Mac and Cheese

"What are you doing?" Came a voice from over their heads
"Who woke me up and why?" growled Gordon, "I had better be at home and you lot better be leaving now so I can sleep"
"I woke you up" said the voice, "I am the Great One, my name is TJ and you are in my cavern"
All their eyes sprung open, even Gordon's, but the light was so bright. They were the brightest lights they had ever seen. They were so bright that all they could see what a bright white ball and nothing else.
"I can't see" said Berti
"Neither can we," said the twins
"TJ is that you?" asked Inspector Sue, whilst shielding her eyes from the light.
"Of course, it is me" replied TJ, "Who else lives in the cavern in the middle of the mountain?"
Inspector Sue tried to see beyond the ball of light to where the voice was coming from, but she could only see a shadow.
"This really is too much" Gordon growled again. "I just want to go home. I want some food. I want mac and cheese with crispy bacon on top and a nice hot cup of tea"
As if by magic a cup of steaming hot tea and a huge bowl of mac and cheese with very crispy bacon appeared in front of Gordon.
"What's this?" Gordon said in surprise.

"You said you wanted mac and cheese with crispy bacon and a cup of tea did you not," said TJ

"Well, yes" replied Gordon, "but I want it in my mound, not here with bright lights in my eyes." He said grumpily.

"TJ, you have to turn these lights down, we cannot see a thing" said Inspector Sue. "You obviously want to talk to us or you wouldn't be here, so can you please turn the lights down so we can talk?" She asked.

"So be it, Farlights back to your walls" TJ commanded and all the Farlights returned to their respective walls and the lighting returned to normal again.

"Farlights?" Said the twins, "what are Farlights?"

"Don't you mean 'Who' are Farlights?" Asked TJ

"We have no idea what we mean, but we also have no idea how we got here or where we are" the twins said, starting to get a little annoyed with this TJ person. "You are talking in riddles" they said, "you are producing food, as if by magic, you are talking to flying lights, this is all simply crazy madness." They paused for a second, "that said, if you could magic us some cheeseburgers and chocolate milkshakes please, it would be really appreciated" the twins said cheekily.

Again, as if by magic, two giant cheeseburgers and two chocolate milkshakes appeared in front of the twins. The cheeseburgers were as big as their heads. Their eyes popped out and then it was like nothing else mattered as they started to munch their way into their burgers.

"Ok come on TJ, you need to tell us what is going

on" said Inspector Sue, who was also starting to lose patience, as TJ just appeared to find this all very funny.
TJ moved round so that he was facing Inspector Sue and Berti, there was no point talking to Gordon or the twins as they were all far too busy eating.
He looked at them both, sat down and another chocolate milkshake appeared in front of him. He picked up the milkshake, took a sip, and began his tale.
"As I believe you already know, many years ago when the dragon was banished from Thunder Mountain two crystal stars where created. The star of KiKo and the star of Thunder. Both the stars were separated. One returned here to the cavern with me and the other to you, Inspector Sue. I have been trapped here ever since. You have had the freedom to go about and grant dreams for anyone that asks." He let out a huge sigh, "that is except for me." He said, "Over and over again, I have dreamt that you will grant my dream to get out of this cavern and to be free, but you have."
Inspector Sue looked confused, "I have never received a dream from you TJ, I promise I haven't. I remember all the dreams that I have ever received and I have never had one from you."
Now it was TJs turn to be confused, every night, since he got trapped in the cavern, he had dreamed getting out. To get out, breathe fresh air and smell things that everyone else took for granted, like the smell of freshly cut grass or fresh paint. How could Inspector Sue have not received

his dream?
Whilst all this has been going on Shelby had been hiding behind a rock, she had not returned to her wall, she wanted to listen and see what was being said.
"Hang on a minute" Shelby cried, "You dreamt of leaving us and not taking us with you."
TJ spun round, "I thought I told you to return to your wall" he shouted in a voice like thunder. "Return to your wall" he said and then took the Star of Thunder from his pocket and turned it to black. He normally kept it on green so that he could fly around the cavern to sit on the top ledge and to talk to the Farlights. The ledge was his favourite place in the cavern. From there he could see everything right across the cavern.
Shelby squealed but refused to go back to her wall. She just sat down in the moss and vanished from TJs sight.
"Who was that?" Berti asked
TJ turned back to Berti and Inspector Sue, "That was Shelby, she is one of the Farlights. She was the first Farlight that I spoke to when I arrived here and she has been my best friend ever since." He explained, "when he Star is on any colour, other than black, I can understand what they say. When it is on black, I just hear squeaks and squeals."
Berti looked to Inspector Sue, this was getting stranger and stranger by the minute. First magic food and flying, glowing Farlights, whatever they were, and now they find out that the Star of Thunder can be used to understand the Farlights.
"Why shout at her then if she's your best friend"

asked Inspector Sue.
"That was not me shouting, that was me telling her that she had disobeyed me. I am the Great One, she must do as I ask. I had asked them all to return to their walls and she disobeyed me." explained TJ.
"So, you're saying that whatever you say has to happen?" Asked Berti who was starting to wonder why TJ had been given any star, never mind one as precious as the Star of Thunder.
"How can I protect them if they do not do as I say?" said TJ, "they need to know that I am here to protect them, I am here to help them get out of here, but I cannot do that if they disobey me."
Inspector Sue looked shocked, "Just because you are here to protect them does not mean that you have to shout at them when they don't do what you want" she said, "You would still be their protector if you didn't shout and didn't get what you want all the time."
TJ looked sad, he knew he was being told off, he had not meant to upset anyone, least of all Shelby. She had always been there for him since he had arrived in the cavern. She had guided him and helped him understand the cavern and its secrets. She had helped him to understand the Star of Thunder and its different powers.
TJ took out the Star of Thunder and turned it back to green. "Shelby" he said "come on, come here, I'm sorry" he said
There was movement in the moss, but Shelby did not appear. "Come on Shelby, I'm sorry" TJ repeated.
The moss moved some more and slowly Shelby

appeared. Her face was red from crying and her cheeks were wet with tears. "I didn't mean to disobey you" she explained, "I just wanted to know everything was ok. I was only here to help and to make sure that you were all right." She said.

"I am sorry" said TJ again, "you have always looked after me and I should have known that is what you were doing."

TJ was interrupted by Gordon who had now finished his cup of tea, and his mac and cheese with crispy bacon and was back to being grumpy again. "This is all well and good," he said, "shout, shout, cry, cry, sorry and more sorrys, but have you forgotten we are here?" He grumbled "You appear to have forgotten that five strangers have just landed in your cavern without a clue what's going on" he said

TJ looked at Gordon, he was a short, rather round little man. It did not surprise TJ that he was so grumpy. If he were so short, he would grumpy too. TJ laughed to himself.

"You think it's funny do you 'O Great One" Gordon shouted, "Well I don't, now tell me how we are getting out of this place."

"Let's all calm down a bit shall we," advised Inspector Sue, "can we let TJ finish explaining everything and then maybe we can make a plan."

TJ tried to remember where he had got up to with his tale. Berti saw that TJ looked a little lost and jumped in to help him, "you got to the point where Inspector Sue had the Star of KiKo, and you were trapped in this cavern with the Star of Thunder and dreaming of getting out." She reminded him.

"Ah yes," said TJ, "you are right. I was here in the cavern with the Star of Thunder. The Star gives me the power to fly, swim and climb as well as making the mountain shake." He explained, "but I still do not know why I need to make the mountain shake. If I am honest, the only reason that I have done it is to try and get your attention Inspector Sue. I have been trying to get my dream of freedom for the Farlights and myself." He paused and looked at Shelby. "I would never leave you behind," he said to her, "I would always take you with me wherever I went."

Shelby smiled and climbed up onto a nearby rock to continue listening.

"You see," TJ continued, "the Farlights have the power to grant you whatever you are thinking, so I have always had food and water and toilet paper, but they can only grant material things, things that actually exist, they cannot grant dreams." TJ paused and looked over to a dark corner of the cavern and sighed, "I even got them to give me a door thinking that if I opened it then it would let me out of here, but it didn't" he said

Inspector Sue was listening intently, and she immediately knew why she had not received TJs dream for freedom. She knew exactly why, but how was she going to help, how was she going to be able to free TJ and the Farlights.

Chapter 8
The Belief

Inspector Sue could only grant dreams that were true of heart and not a reward for the person requesting the dream. She knew that was why she had never received TJ's dream.
His dream was purely about himself, even though he told Shelby that he would take the Farlights with him, she knew, from what he had said, that he had only dreamt of his own freedom and not of anyone else's. So, whilst, in his heart of hearts he may have genuinely wanted to escape the cavern, it was definitely a reward for himself and that was why his dream had never made it to the dream door.
The issue that Inspector Sue now had was how she could help.
She could not tell TJ that was why she had not received his dream. Inspector Sue had learnt over the years that if she told someone how to get a dream, they would also not come to the dream door, as they would not be true of heart. She had to find a way for TJ or one of the Farlights to dream a dream that was true of heart and not a reward for themselves, but how was she going to do it she wondered.
Berti interrupted her thoughts "but if you got in here TJ, there must be a way out." She said, "how did you get in?"
"The same way you did" replied TJ, "the star brought me here."

He sat back down and picked up his milkshake, which was nearly empty, but still, he threw it across the cavern. "I just don't understand" he cried, "I was always good, I always looked after my brothers, I always did as I was told, so why am I here? What did I do?"
The cavern fell silent, even the twins stopped munching their burgers and slurping their chocolate shakes and everyone looked at TJ.
"You didn't do anything wrong" Inspector Sue said, "none of us did, we are the chosen ones, we are the ones chosen by the stars to help those that need it." She explained.
Gordon suddenly stood up, puffed out his chest and cleared his throat, "ahem, this is getting us nowhere, we need to think about this." He said, "If we really are the chosen ones then we are here for a reason. There is a reason that we ended up at the top of the biggest tree, with the biggest trunk and the highest branches tonight. There is a reason TJ got the Star of Thunder and ended up here in the cavern with the Farlights. There is a reason that TJ chose tonight to shake the mountain. There is a reason that we all put our stars together to end up in this cavern. There is a reason for everything and I believe in fate. I believe that everything happens for a reason and whilst, yes, I can be grumpy, this is because fate has never been kind to me." At this point he paused. Everyone in the cavern was looking at him, even all the Farlights were looking at him.
"So, what are you thinking?" asked Berti, curious to work out why Gordon had suddenly turned from being extremely grumpy to being the voice of

reason.
Gordon continued, “well I have been thinking,” He always did all his best thinking after he had eaten, “I have been thinking that we need to look at this step by step and I believe the answer is in there somewhere.” He paused again, he was hoping someone else would have thought the same as him or, at the very least, joined him on his thought train, as this was the end of the line of his thought train. He had not thought any further than this, but he was utterly convinced that this was all happening for a reason, they just had to work out why.
“So, let’s look at the facts” said Inspector Sue, “Berti and I got our stars when we were dreaming of helping people when we had no one to help” TJ jumped up, “So why didn’t you help me, why didn’t you grant my dream?” He asked. Gordon cut him off, “TJ, we are looking at the facts, we will get nowhere if you keep going on about your own dreams. Continue with the facts please Inspector Sue.”
Everyone’s attention turned back to Inspector Sue. She looked around the cavern, she wished she knew the answer, she wished she knew how to help everyone. All the faces looking up at her expected an answer, but she did not know what it was. She was always the one people went to for the answers and normally she always had them, only this time she did not. “Pull yourself together” she said, not realising that she had said it aloud, “ok, let us look at the facts. Berti and I got our stars whilst dreaming of helping others when we had no one to help. TJ how did you get your star?”

she asked.
TJ looked back at her and thought for a moment.
"I was out walking one night; I always went for a walk when I was annoyed," TJ said.
"Why were you annoyed" asked the twins.
TJ had to think for a moment as it had been a long time since he had thought about why he was annoyed. "Oh, I remember," he said, "I had been out with my brothers that evening and my younger brother had fallen down a hill and hurt himself. I took him home and mummy blamed me for him hurting himself, but it was not my fault. He just slipped and fell, there was nothing I could do about it. I wished there were something I could have done to protect him from falling, but I could not." He paused and looked up to the ceiling of the cavern. He was not sure what this had to do with why he was here. Had he been banished here because he did not protect his brother? He was starting to feel confused.
"Just sit down and breath" said Inspector Sue, "it can be hard remembering things from so long ago."
TJ was thankful for the little sit down, but he wanted to understand, so he knew he had to continue.
"So, after mum had shouted at me, I went out for a walk. I walked all the way to the moor and across to the lake. I loved the lake, I used to always go there to think. I walked out onto the bridge and sat down in the middle of it. I was gazing into the lake thinking about my brothers and how much I loved them and wanted to protect them and then the next thing I knew I was here

in the cavern."
A smile spread across Inspector Sue's face, "so there is answer number one," she said, "Berti and I were dreaming of helping people and you, TJ, we're thinking of protecting your brothers, so we got the KiKo stars that grant dreams to help people and you got the Star of Thunder that protects people" she explained.
"But who am I protecting in here" asked TJ, "I can't get out of here to protect anyone or anything, so I'm not sure you are right." He said.
"What about us and the treasure?" Said Shelby
TJ thought for a moment, yes, he had been looking after the Farlights and the treasure, but no one else knew about the treasure or the Farlights so that was not hard.
"You have a point Shelby," he said, "but if no one knows about you or the treasure why does it need protecting?"
The twins jumped in, "And that still doesn't explain why we are here,"
"One step at a time" said Berti who was getting a little annoyed by all the interruptions. "We need to work through this so we understand why everything happened and then, like Gordon said, we will find the answer."
"We also know that Gordon and the twins got their stars as part of my dream" said Inspector Sue.
"But why us? Why not anyone else?" Asked the twins
"That is a good question" said Berti, "we know why TJ, Inspector Sue and I got our stars but the other three Stars of KiKo could have gone to

anyone, why Gordon and the twins?"
"Let's start with the twins" said Inspector Sue, "what were you doing or thinking when you got your Stars?"
The twins lay back in the soft moss and looked about the sparkling walls. What were they thinking? What were they doing? Terry suddenly jumped up and for the first time he spoke on his own, "I remember," He shouted. "I remember what we were doing." He looked at Toby and then Toby jumped up as well. "Me too." Shouted Toby and then, just like that they were talking at the same time again. "We had just made some hot scones with strawberry jam and really thick cream to celebrate our day. You see we had been out and about, like we do, and we came across a dog on a long chain but it was loose in a car park. It was such a lovely dog, she was a big, black Labrador called Bella. We could not see an owner and so we found out who her owner was and we returned her. It made us feel good that we had helped someone. We had done something for someone without being asked and without any reward to ourselves. So, we made our own reward and made hot scones with jam and cream, which is our favourite treat."
Gordon jumped in, "so you did something pure of heart and did not expect a reward, maybe that was why you were picked, but I am still trying to remember why I would have been chosen."
"Maybe you need to relax," said Berti, "it is getting serious right now, so I can imagine it is hard to think. Why don't we all have a sit down or a walk about and a drink and it may come back

to you." She said.
Gordon knew that he thought better after food, "maybe, if I had another cup of tea and maybe some pancakes with chocolate spread, it may help me to think."
"This is a most excellent idea," announced TJ, who was always hungry and loved a chocolate milkshake. "Everyone think of their favourite food and drink, the Farlights will bring it to you." He said
"Let's have a break" said Berti "and come back together in half an hour. We could be here a while, so everyone get something to eat please"
As each of them thought of their favourite food it appeared in front of them. Inspector Sue got a mint choc chip ice cream sundae and a strawberry milkshake. Berti got carrot cake and apple juice. The twins got hot scones, jam and cream. TJ and Gordon both got big fluffy pancakes and chocolate spread.
Everyone sat down and tucked into their food. The cavern fell silent as everyone ate and they thought about why they were here with everyone else.
Inspector Sue loved mint choc chip ice cream, it was her most favourite food in the world, if you can call ice cream, food. As she ate, she thought about all the facts, but no matter how she thought of them, she could not see a way out of the cavern. They had already tried putting all the Stars of KiKo together and they went nowhere. Maybe there was somewhere they needed to put the Stars, maybe it was something to do with the treasure.

Berti wandered over to Inspector Sue with her carrot cake, “You are thinking over the facts, aren’t you?” she asked. Inspector Sue nodded.
“Me too.” Said Berti, “We need to know how Gordon got his star. Maybe that will help us”
As Gordon speared the last piece of his pancakes and wiped it around the plate to get every bit of the chocolate spread it came to him, he knew why he had been picked.

Chapter 9
The Revelation

Gordon slowly chewed his last piece of pancake and thought carefully, should he tell everyone what he thought the reason was that he had been picked. He had never told anyone this before, he was in fact a little scared to tell them. He finally swallowed his last piece of, very well chewed, pancake, took a sip of his tea and stood up. He was not sure he could do this, but if it meant that he got home then he was going to have to.

"I think I know why I was chosen" he announced to the group. Everyone turned to look at him and this made him feel very self-conscience, now he was even more scared to tell them as they were all looking, staring even, at him in expectation of the reason.

"Are you going to tell us then?" Asked the twins.

"Yes, Yes, I'm going to tell you, but this is not easy for me, so please bare with me." Gordon said and with that he took a final sip of his tea and began his story.

"I have not always been so grumpy, in fact I am not really grumpy at all, I just pretend," he said, "You see many years ago, when I was younger, I had a girlfriend called Glinda. She was beautiful and funny, kind and caring. She had long curly blonde hair and a laugh that sounded like bells." He paused as he remembered just how beautiful Glinda was and how much he had loved her. "One

day the dragon that lived in the Mountain came and took her away. There was nothing I could do, he just swooped down, grabbed her with his giant claws and flew off back to the mountain.
For months and months, I tried to find a way into the mountain to rescue her, but I just could not find a way in. Then came the dreadful, dreadful night that the villagers blew up the mountain. I pleaded with them not to do it, I begged, but they would not listen, they did it anyway.
The fire was so hot I could not get near, I tried, I tried so hard, but I burnt my beard and my hat and I just had to come away. I waited until the fire had gone out and then I searched for days, hoping that she had found a way out, but eventually I had to give up." Gordon stopped and wiped a tear from his eye.
He could still see Glinda, as she was on the day that she was taken, all those years before. He still missed her so much; it was like a piece of him was missing.
Berti passed Gordon a tissue, "Are you ok?" She asked
"Yes, yes" replied Gordon, "I have just never told anyone this story before and I miss her so much." He paused again for another sip of tea and continued, "ever since that day I have kept myself to myself, I didn't want to make any new friends in case someone or something took them away. Whenever anyone has tried to be my friend, I have always been grumpy so that they would not stay and they would not want to be my friend. That way I cannot get hurt again.
Last night, before I was woken by the star hitting

me on the head, I dreamt that I helped someone. I did not want them to be my friend, but I helped them anyway. They were stuck in the lake and could not get out. I did not know who it was, but I waded in as deep as I could and I helped pull them to safety. It made me happy. In my dream I wanted to help more people, but I did not want them as my friends."

Berti smiled at Gordon, "so you were dreaming about wanting to help people, you were showing pureness of heart. You did not want their friendship or a reward, which sounds like the right reasons to get a Star of KiKo to me, don't you think Inspector Sue?"

Inspector Sue nodded, "I do indeed, that is a very good reason" she said.

"What was that?" said the twins who had moved and were now leaning against one of the cavern walls, "We felt a drop of water on our heads"

TJ laughed, "You're in a cavern, they do have a tendency to drip every now and again" he explained.

"No, this wasn't a cavern drip, this was different, we know it was." The twins replied looking confused.

TJ laughed again, "How is a drip not a drip?" He asked

"We don't know, it felt like water, but it wasn't like a drip that lands 'splash' on you, but more like glitter or dust"

Shelby, who had still been sat on the rock near TJ, flew over to the twins.

"Where exactly were you stood" she asked

The twins looked at each other, "We were here, we

haven't moved" they said and then stamped their little feet, as if to make the point that they had not moved.

Shelby looked up the wall of the cavern to where there was a Farlight hole. It was up near the top of the wall, almost where it joined with the ceiling. She flew up the wall and hovered just outside the front of the hole. The Farlights light was dim and there was sniffling coming from the hole.

Shelby knew all the Farlights in the cavern "Sandra, are you ok?" She asked quietly

"Go away" came a tiny voice from the back of the hole.

"Sandra, what is the matter, please come out and speak to me. I know all this is very confusing, but we will work it out, I promise" said Shelby in her most convincing voice. She was not sure they would work it out, but she knew they would try their best.

Slowly Sandra walked out to the front of her hole.

"I am sure my name is not really Sandra, it is Glinda. The Glinda that Gordon is speaking of is me. I am the one that was taken by the dragon, I am the reason that he is grumpy" she said, and she started to cry again.

"I didn't know until just now, when I heard his story, and suddenly it all came back to me. My name is Glinda, I was taken by the dragon and brought to the cavern" Sandra sniveled again.

Shelby did not understand, how could Glinda be Sandra? Sandra had always been a Farlight, she could not be Glinda.

Farlights only existed in the cavern, or so Shelby thought, and then she remembered. It came back

to her like a flash of light, she was not called Shelby, she was called Shelly. She also remembered being taken by the dragon.
Could all the Farlights have been taken by the dragon? Could they have survived the fire and if they did how did they survive? How did they become Farlights?
This night was getting increasingly confusing by the minute. There were certainly more questions than answers right now.
"Come on" said Shelby, "we need to tell them."
Together Shelby and Sandra flew back down to where the others where all waiting.
As Shelby and Sandra landed, all the other Farlights started to come down from their holes and formed a ring around the others. One side of the ring parted and Victor and Vicky flew into the centre.
"We knew this day would come," said Victor.
He turned to Vicky who was looking around all the other Farlights, "We knew it would come when all the stars were back together" she said.
"What would come?" Asked TJ, who was now totally lost with what was going on.
"Your future" said Vicky and Victor together.

Chapter 10
The Treasure

Victor took another step forward, "The stories that you have heard are mostly true, but there are some parts that we may have misled you or we did not tell you." He took a breather and looked across at Vicky who nodded and smiled a sad smile, as he continued "You see all those years ago when the dragon was here in this cavern, he would bring all his treasure back here to hide it. Treasure could be anything bright and shiny and that included anyone that was bright and shiny. He did not separate material things like gold and gems from those, like Shelby and Sandra. If they had a bright and shiny personality, they were as precious to him as gold and gems."

He looked about the cavern and everyone was staring at him, totally mesmerised with this latest information. There was not a sound except the running of the waterfall and the stream.

"Go on," said Vicky, "they are listening, you have to tell them now."

Victor smiled at Vicky and continued, "You see, Vicky and I were here with the dragon. We were far too small to stop him, but we could look after all his treasure. We made sure that any treasure that he brought back, that needed food or drinks, had whatever they wanted." As he said this, all the Farlights must have been thinking of their

favourite food as they all suddenly had food in front of them, but they were all listening so intently that none of them noticed the food.
"When the explosion happened, Vicky and I tied to save what we could. We grabbed whatever we could, that had not already melted, and we threw it into the stream. All the actual treasure sank, but all the people that the dragon had taken could not hide under the water as they would not be able to breathe. Vicky and I decided, there and then, that the only way we could save them, was to put a spell on them all. So we turned them all into golden Farlights."
Victor sat down on a nearby rock. He knew that one day he would have to tell them all this story. He just hoped that they would all understand why they had done what they did. He looked across the cavern at the Farlights, they were all just sat, staring back at him, in disbelief.
Vicky knew that Victor was struggling to tell this story "We did this to save you all," She said, "If we had not turned you into Farlights and given you the power to swim under the waterfall you would not have survived the fire."
Victor continued "We thought that once the dragon was gone, we would be able to fly out of the cavern and then we could turn you back to who you were." He rubbed his eyes and sighed. "But when the dragon was gone"' he said, "and the flames had all died down the mountain was sealed closed. We could not get out and we were left with a pool of gold and two crystal gems. We tried to touch the gems, but we could not get anywhere near them. Then one day the gems

vanished and a vision appeared in the gold. The white gem was pure and clear, as I have told you before, we called this the star of KiKo, as that is white in Farlish. The other we called the Star of Thunder, as every now and then, it would glow and make a loud sound like thunder.
In the vision we saw that the Star of KiKo had gone to a lady who was strict, clever and kind. Someone that wanted to help others. She was as pure as the Star was white.
We did not see where the other star had gone for some time and it did not look like the lady was coming to save us." Victor stopped again.
Shelby stood up, "So are you telling me that we are not really Farlights?" She asked
Vicky turned to look at her and smiled gently, "As it looked like no one was coming to save us, it was then, that Victor and I decided that you would be better off being Farlights until we could work out how to get you out of here."
Victor took over the story, "So we gave you all new names that, as you know, all start with S. We decided that they should be S's as you were all so special" he stopped for a moment and looked across to all the Farlights. "We dreamed that one day our wishes would come true that we would be able to get all you all out of the mountain and turn you back to yourselves."
TJ coughed, "And then I arrived?" He asked.
"Yes" said Vicky, "That very night you appeared and we thought our dreams had come true."
"But we are still here," said TJ
"Yes, yes you are, but we needed both the stars together. Now that we have the Star of KiKo and

the Star of Thunder together you must be able to find a way out." Victor said.
All the Farlights, except Shelby, had been quiet until now. Suddenly they all started asking questions at the same time. Who were they really? Where did they live before the dragon took them? What were their real names?
"QUIETTTT" shouted TJ, "This is all a lot of information to take in for everyone, but we need to listen and understand all of this, so we can work out how to get us all out of here."
The cavern fell quiet again.
"Can I ask," said Gordon, "We know where the crystals are, but where is the gold?"
"The gold" said TJ, "is all at the bottom of the waterfall. When I arrived the Farlights showed me how to use the Star of Thunder so that I could swim under the water and down to the gold at the bottom of the waterfall. That is where it is hidden, it was all put there after the fire. It is now three giant pools of gold that are stacked on top of each other under the water. If you look very closely you can see the gold glistening."
Gordon and the twins immediately ran to the waterfall and looked down into the water, but all they could see were bubbles. Toby lay down on the edge of the moss and peered closer at the water, he thought he saw a flash of gold. "Come here" he said to Terry.
"What have you seen? Have you seen the gold?" Asked Terry.
Toby looked up at Terry, "I am not sure, I may have. Come on, look."
They both lay on the moss, side by side and

peered into the water. They got so close to the water that they were touching the water with their noses. They looked at each other, took a deep breath and stuck their heads under the water.
As they both opened their eyes and looked around under the water. They could not see anything, there were just too many bubbles from the waterfall.
They came back up and lay on the moss. “There is nothing down there” They both said.
While they were under the water TJ had walked over to the waterfall. “Do you really think that it would be hidden where you can see it?” He laughed, “it is far, far down and hidden in a cave behind the sheet of water that is the waterfall. You would not be able to swim to it, but this is not getting us out of here is it? Come on, we need to figure this out.”
As they all walked back to the rest of the group Gordon felt that TJ was hiding something. He did not know what, but something told him that something was not right.

Chapter 11
The Idea

Whilst the others had been over at the waterfall all the Farlights had started to ask their questions again. Inspector Sue moved away from the group and began looking at the Star of KiKo again.
Over the years she had studied the Star many, many times but for some reason, today it looked different. She was not sure, but she thought that it was glowing brighter than normal. It had a slight tinge of green, blue and purple running through the middle like a rainbow. She turned it over and over in her hands and thought to herself, I have a Star of KiKo and so do Berti, Gordon and the twins. TJ has a Star of Thunder, which was six stars in total, but if there was more than one Star of KiKo, were there more Stars of Thunder?
There had to be a link between the Stars. They must have all been formed at the same time, or were they? Victor had only said that there was two Stars created, so if that was the case, where did the other four come from? Had the extra four stars also been created in the fire? Had they vanished before they were found? No, that could not be right. It had been years since she got her star and the others had only got theirs tonight. So where did they come from?
She needed to get all the Stars together and see if they matched hers but how was she going to get

them.
As the others returned to the group, Inspector Sue made her way back as well.
Gordon made his way straight to Inspector Sue and Berti. “I don’t think there is any gold” he grumbled. “The twins couldn’t see any. I don’t trust TJ and these Farlights, something doesn’t seem right” he said
Inspector Sue studied Gordon for a moment “I do not see why we should not trust them; they are trapped in here as much as we are. They want to get out as much as we do. They have no reason to tell us lies” she said.
“Oh, I don’t know” said Gordon, “Victor and Vicky turning them all into Farlights and not telling them all this time. What would you be thinking if you were one of them? They have been living a lie”
“That maybe so” said Berti, “But as Inspector Sue said, they have no reason to tell us lies. They obviously have magical powers as they have brought us all this food, which, I may add, was absolutely delicious.”
“I can’t be bought with food,” said Gordon “although I do agree, it was amazing food, but that aside I still don’t trust them.”
“I’ve got an idea” said Inspector Sue, “Come with me”
Inspector Sue, Berti and Gordon re-joined the main group and she climbed up onto one of the rocks. “SILENCE PLEASE” she said in a loud and authoritative voice.

The voices around the cavern stared to die down "SILENCE" shouted TJ. "You have something to say Inspector Sue"

"I have an idea" Inspector Sue said, "it may not do anything, but I want to try something."

TJ was curious as to what Inspector Sue's idea would be, "so what's your idea" he asked.

Inspector Sue took out her Star of KiKo, turned it over in her hand and then looked back across at TJ. "Each of the stars has six sides and we have six stars" she said, "I think that we need to put them all together. We need to match all the sides together and see what happens"

"I think the Inspector has a good idea there" said Gordon, "if we put them all back together, it may get us out of here. Come on everyone get out your stars"

"Hold it right there" said TJ, "I do not understand, how do they fit together? Which order do they go in?"

"No one knows" said Gordon, "but it's an idea and I think we should try it, so everyone get their Stars out and let us put them together"

Gordon had found a large flat rock and he took out his star. Berti, the twins and Inspector Sue joined him at the rock, however TJ remained still.

"Are you coming?" Berti shouted across to TJ

TJ just stood and stared back at them; he just did not know if this was the right thing to do. "What if it doesn't work?" he asked

"We won't know if we don't try" said Berti "Now

come, join us and let us give this a go"
TJ thought for a moment and then decided that even if there was only a tiny chance that this would work, he was willing to try. He slowly walked over to them and took out his Star.
"How are they fitting together?" Asked the twins
"Well, there are six sides and six stars so let's try them side by side first" suggested Berti.
Everyone laid their stars on the rock so they were in a line touching each other. They all stared at the Stars. Nothing was happening. "Well, that didn't do anything" grumbled Gordon.
"What about putting them together at their ends to make a star. Six sides on each Star, so it would make a six-pointed star." Suggested Inspector Sue
"Ooooo" Said the Twins, "We like that idea"
Again, they all laid their Stars on the rock, but this time in the shape of a Star with all their points touching.
They stood back, but again, nothing happened.
"Maybe we have to be holding them" suggested TJ.
They all picked up their Stars and held them together in a line and held their breath. Again, nothing happened.
"O this is useless, it didn't work, we are never getting out of here," cried the twins
"We can't give up" said Inspector Sue "there must be an answer here somewhere. Let us just take a break, we have all taken in a lot of information

today. I don't know about anyone else, but I am so tired. I think we need to have a nap and then we can come back together with fresh minds and try again."

For the first time in a while Gordon smiled, he was certainly tired and whilst he could not wait to get back to his mound, he knew that they would all feel better if they had a sleep.

"There are lots of little caves off the cavern that you can use as bedrooms" TJ said. "They are very comfy and I could do with a sleep as well" TJ took off towards the top of the cavern to his ledge and all the Farlights returned to their walls.

"I guess we are just finding the caves for ourselves then" said Berti with a smile and with that they all went in different directions to find themselves a cave.

Chapter 12
The Truth

Berti had found a lovely cave with thick green moss and it even had a little mound that she could use as a pillow.
She settled down; she was so tired but she was starting to get cold. She wished she had a blanket or a duvet to warm her up like she had in her burrow at home. Then, as if by magic, she had the warmest, snuggest duvet laid over the top of her.
She then remembered what the Farlights had said about wishing for material items.
Everything that had happened over the last few hours was a lot to take in but right now she was just too tired to think about it anymore. So, she closed her eyes, snuggled down and went to sleep.
The twins and Gordon had also found their caves and were tucked up tight and fast asleep.
Inspector Sue had found a cave, she had tried to sleep but she could not. She could not stop going over everything that had happened since the four shadows had arrived on her platform. The joining of their four crystals, landing in the cavern, meeting TJ and the Farlights. Then finally realising that they were trapped. How could this be possible when all she ever did was help people, she granted their dreams by helping them understand how to make their own dream come

true.
She lay back down on the soft moss and ran through all the events of the day again and again but still no answers came to her. She was missing something, but what, what was she missing. There was something she did not know, something that would complete the puzzle. She played it over and over in her mind and eventually sleep took over and fell into a deep restless sleep.
Once everyone was asleep in their caves and the Farlights had all returned to their walls. The cavern was quiet and Vicky and Victor quietly made their way back out to the waterfall.
"This is our chance to free them all" whispered Vicky
Victor did not look convinced. He knew she was right and this was what they had agreed all those years ago when the dragon left. They had agreed that they would do whatever was needed to get the Farlights back to their families and friends. However now, that it was a potential reality, he was not sure he wanted it to happen.
Before the fire and the Farlights, Vicky and Victor had been alone with the dragon. They had been cursed to live forever in the cavern. The only way that they could be freed was if the dragon left the cavern forever.
Together they worked hard to do whatever they could to stop the dragon from going to Fluffington. They had tried many times to get the dragon to leave, but it never worked. They tried to

keep him happy. They sang him lullabies to send him to sleep and they brought him food when he was angry. They did everything they could to stop him going to the town, but it was a real challenge. When the fire had started, they knew it was their chance to get away, but they could not leave all the ones that the dragon had taken. They did not care about the treasure, but they had to make sure that the others were all safe.

They convinced the dragon that the villagers were coming to get him and that he had to get away or he would die. The dragon believed them and took off through the top of the mountain. As he flew out, he caved in the only exit, trapping Vicky and Victor in the cavern. Their escape route was blocked.

They had to do something, they had to save the others. They did the only thing they could do, they put the spell on everyone to turn them into Farlights. As Farlights they were tiny, they could fly and they could breathe under the water.

Vicky took everyone to the secret cave behind the waterfall. It was way down deep below the surface of the water in the pool behind the falls. In the meantime, Victor put a spell on the melted treasure to form a shield over the waterfall to protect them from the fire.

As the shield was created over Victor's head, all the crystals dropped down and welded together creating one giant crystal and a shield of solid gold. As the giant crystal hit the water it shattered into seven identical pieces. Each was exactly the same except one. Six were perfectly clear but the seventh was multicoloured.

Victor didn't have time to think, he collected them all together and hid them in his pockets. He then dove down behind the waterfall to join the others in the secret cave.

Every few hours Victor would swim up to the surface to see if the air in the dome has cooled down. It took eight days for the temperature to come down low enough for them all to surface.

Before Victor returned to tell the others that they could surface, he put two of the crystals on the ground near the edge of the gold dome. He laid one of the clear crystals and the multicoloured one on the ground and put a different spell on each. The spell on the clear one meant that it could only be held by someone that was pure of heart and did not seek rewards. The spell on the multicoloured one meant that it could only be held by a protector.

He then dove back down to tell the others they could come to the surface. Before he left the secret cave, he carved a hole in the wall and hid the other five crystals. Only he and Vicky knew they were there.

Once they had all returned to the surface, they turned the gold dome into three giant, coin shaped, pieces of gold. They then used them to close the entrance to the cave and put a spell on them so that they could not be moved. They had remained there until now as the guarded secret of the Farlights. The other Farlights all knew the treasure was hidden in the cave behind the gold, but they did not know what it was.

"We have to go and get the seventh crystal" Vicky whispered. "They have worked out that they need to put their crystals together but they need the seventh one to complete it"

"I know, I know" said Victor "It's just going to be so quiet here when they all leave"

"We don't know they will go" said Vicky kindly, "Some of them may stay. Now come on, let us get that crystal."

Vicky and Victor held hands and dove down under the waterfall and down to the cave at the bottom of the pool.

They broke the spell that held the three giant gold coins in place and guarded the entrance to the cave. They swam in and over to the hole in the wall where the seventh crystal was hidden.

Vicky reached in and carefully removed the crystal. She looked across at Victor and then together they swam back up to the surface.

The cavern was still quiet and Vicky and Victor flew and sat on the rock at the centre of the cavern, in the centre of the stream, under the bridge.

"As soon as they wake, we give them the seventh crystal," said Vicky

Victor still did not look convinced "Do we have to give it to them? Could they not find it

somewhere?" He said, "The Farlights are already angry with us for not telling them where they came from. They need to work this out themselves. I let two of the crystals go and that stopped us from putting them all back together."
Vicky squeezed his hand "we have the chance to do the right thing and help, not only everyone here in the cavern, but hundreds and hundreds of others once they can get out of here."

"I know, I know" replied Victor, "but they are our family, I don't want to lose them."

"We will never lose them" insisted Vicky, "as you say, they are our family and no matter how angry or happy we are, no matter how far apart we are, we will always be family. Let us leave the crystal here on this rock and get some sleep. When they are all up, they will find the crystal and I just know they will work it out."

With that Vicky and Victor flew up to their own cave high on the wall of the cavern and went to sleep.

Chapter 13
The Colours

Inspector Sue was the first to reappear in the main cavern, she had not slept well, or for very long. She was hungry and she wished for some fresh fruit and yogurt and as expected, it appeared in front of her. As she sat down on a rock, near the stream, to eat her fruit and yogurt and the smell of crispy bacon wafted through the cavern. Someone was having bacon, Inspector Sue loved bacon, especially crispy bacon, but today she wanted fruit. She needed a clear head today to work on a plan to get everyone out of here.

She finished her fruit and yogurt and got up to walk around the cavern. It still amazed her how soft the moss was under her feet. She had taken her shoes and socks off before she went to bed but had not put them back on when she woke, as the moss was just so comfortable to walk on.

She wandered across to the waterfall and stood right on the edge of the pool where the waterfall landed. She could feel the spray of the waterfall on her face and it was so cool and refreshing. She sat down, the moss was very damp, but she did not care. She dipped her toes into the pool and it was just so nice to feel the water running over her

feet. She put her arms out behind her and stretched out.
It was so quiet, just the sound of the running water and the cool spray from the waterfall, it was so relaxing.
She looked up the waterfall and across the ceiling of the cavern at the glistening blue/green crystals, then back to the waterfall. She followed the running water down the waterfall, across her feet and on down the river to the bridge. As she watched the water run round both sides of the giant rock that was under the bridge something, on top of the rock, caught her eye.
There was a Star on there. Whose Star was it? Had one of the others left theirs there?
She jumped up and hurried across to the bridge. The water in the stream was not that deep, so she carefully stepped into the stream and step by step got closer to the rock.
She bent over as she got nearer the rock so she didn't bang her head on the bottom of the bridge. She reached forward towards the Star. Slowly she picked it up and turned it over in her hand. It was just the same as her Star, she placed it gently in her pocket and gingerly picked her way back to the bank of the stream and sat down on the edge. She took the Star from her pocket and then took her own Star from her other pocket and put them side by side. Nothing happened but as she looked at them the green, blue and purple tinge that she had seen before on her Star got brighter. The

other Star did the same, but it had different colours. The colours on the other one were yellow, red and black. She had to wake the others, she had to know if this was a new Star of one of the existing ones they knew about.
She quickly and quietly ran from cave to cave to find them all and wake them up. After about ten minutes she had them all back together.
Gordon was none too pleased to have been woken up again, but when Inspector Sue said that she had found another crystal he softened a little.
"Has everyone got their crystals? Please show them to me" she said. She had already prepared herself for one of them to say that theirs was missing but none of them did. They all produced their Stars and each had a different combination of colours.
Now there were seven stars all with a different colour and they still had no clue how the Stars could help them.
"I am sure this is a puzzle" she said, "we must piece them together in the right order. Mine has green, blue and purple. The new one has yellow, red and black. What colours do you have?"
Gordon turned his over in his hand, "mine has blue, purple and yellow"
"Mine has purple, yellow and red" said Terry and Toby followed with "mine has black, green and blue"
Berti was thinking how this would work, she was not really listening to the others, she was trying

to understand how the colours mattered.
"Berti, are you listening" asked Inspector Sue
Berti jumped, she had been miles away, "sorry, mine has red, black and green" she said quite embarrassed that she had been caught not listening.
"But we all have three colours" said the twins, "how do we know which goes with which"
TJ had been quiet until now, he had been thinking and he was sure he had the answer. "I think I know" he said, "my crystal has six colours, one on each side. I think we need to match colours from your crystals to the colours on mine. We now have six white crystals, so that is one for each side of my crystal. So, I think that mine goes in the middle and yours all fit around the outside."
Far above them Vicky and Victor were watching from their cave.
"I told you they would work it out," said Vicky
Victor screwed up his face, "now to see what happens" he said.
"So how do we do this?" Asked Berti, "How do we work out where they all go? Do we hold them all together or do we balance them on the rock again?"
"I think" said TJ, "that we need to work out which goes where and then I will hold up my Star as the centre and you then push yours up against mine."
"Do we do it one at a time or all together?" Asked the twins

"I would suggest all at the same time" said Berti. Inspector Sue had been thinking. "I think I've got it" she said. "We all have three colours; I think we need to look at the order of the colours on TJ's crystal and then match the middle colour from our crystals to his"

The others thought for a second, "I think she is right" said Gordon, "What is the order of the colours TJ?"

"Ok, start at green," said TJ

"Who has green as their middle colour" asked Gordon

Toby stuck his crystal in the air "that would be me"

"Ok, so you are green, that's number one" said Gordon, "what is the next colour TJ?"

"It's Green and then Blue" TJ replied

Immediately Inspector Sue raised her crystal, "I have Blue" she said

"Next comes Purple," said TJ

"That's mine" said Gordon

"Then yellow," said TJ

Up shot Terry's hand waving his crystal about madly. "Me" he shouted excitedly

"Then red," said TJ

Inspector Sue put her hand up again, "That's the new one" she said

"And finally black which must be Berti's as she is the only one left" said TJ "so that is all of them. As each crystal has three colours you must make sure that you have your crystal the right way up

so the colours either side match the colours next to them. Remember the colours are Green, Blue, Purple, Yellow, Red and Black, in that order" he said, "ok are we all ready? I shall raise my crystal up and then on the count of three you must all place yours on the corresponding colour. Everyone move to your places and get ready."
Everyone shuffled around so that they were in the right order and TJ knelt on the ground so everyone could reach his crystal.
"Are we ready" TJ asked
"As ready as we will ever be" said Gordon
TJ counted down, "Three, Two, One, Go" and on Go everyone stepped forward and placed their crystal against TJ's on the corresponding colour. They waited and they waited, but nothing happened.
"You have to be kidding me" said Gordon, "I was sure this would work"
TJ looked up from beneath his crystal. "Hang on a minute," he said, "Terry your crystal is upside down, your colours are not matching you goof. No wonder nothing happened."
Gordon looked like he was going to tear Terry limb from limb, he was not sure how much more he could take and he was starting to get hungry and sleepy again.
"Everyone remove your crystals and let's go again" said TJ, "Ready? Three, Two, One, Go"

Chapter 14
The Crystal

They all placed their crystals up against TJs and as soon that they all touched, they started to get hot. They got so hot they could not hold them and had to let go.

As they let go, the crystals, locked together to create one giant crystal which floated in the air between them. All seven pieces just hung their getting hotter and hotter. All the white crystals were glowing brightly with the colour that they had been matched to on TJ's Star. The giant crystal was sending a stream of colour up to the ceiling.

The Farlights had all left their walls to come down and see what was happening, however Vicky and Victor stayed up in their hole and watched.

The streams of light got hotter and hotter and then brighter and brighter until everyone had to step away from the crystal and shield their eyes from the light.

"What's happening?" cried the twins

"Absolutely no idea," said TJ

Suddenly the big coins of gold rose out from under the waterfall and made a column around the crystals and the beams of light. The column went from the floor of the cavern right up to the

roof and the temperature in the cavern immediately dropped and returned to normal.
"What do we do now?" Berti asked.
She was not sure who she was asking, as she knew that no one knew the answer. As expected, her question was answered with silence.
After a few minutes Gordon stepped forward, "so I'm guessing this has to mean something" he said.
TJ moved forward towards the column of gold. As he got closer, he noticed a line in the side of the column. He ran his finger down it, the column was cold. As he moved his finger sparks flew off the column and a door opened.
TJ took a huge step back expecting the heat from the crystals to blast him in the face, but instead the smell of freshly cut grass blew in his face. He took a step closer to the door and peered inside the column.
"What is it?" Asked Berti, "what's in there?"
The inside of the column was bright with sunlight, he looked up and saw the sky. He let out a scream, he had not seen the sky for so long.
"Come look, come look" he shouted, "I can see the sky"
The others ran over to the door and hustled to try and see inside the column, they all gasped.
"But how do we get up there?" Asked Inspector Sue.
"We can fly up and have a look" volunteered the twins and without waiting for an answer, they both shot up the inside of the column to the top

and disappeared out of sight.
A few seconds later they reappeared and flew back down into the cavern. "It's a way out, the column comes out at the top of the mountain."
Cheers echoed around the cavern. They finally had a way out, but how were those that could not fly to get out.
"I want to try something" said TJ, "everyone out of the column"
Once everyone was out of the column TJ stepped back into the column and closed the door. He ran his finger up the seam on the inside of the column that went all the way to the top and as he did, he floated up to the surface.
Once he was at the top, he ran his finger down the seam and he floated back down.
He opened the door at the bottom and stepped out onto the cavern.
"We have a route out" he announced, "We can leave"
It was then that Vicky and Victor flew down from their hole.
"It is time," said Victor
Everyone looked at him, "time for what?" Said TJ
"It's time to turn the Farlights back to who they were" Vicky said, "we promised we would return them to themselves once we had a way out and now you do."
Victor blinked his eyes twice, winked with his left eye and tapped his right foot twice and just like that, all the Farlights returned to who they were

before the fire.
"Glinda" shouted Gordon, tears welling up in his eyes, "Is that you?"
Glinda ran across the cavern and straight to Gordon. "What are we doing in here?" She asked
Victor whispered in Gordon's ear, "She doesn't remember anything" he said
Gordon nodded and looked at Glinda, "we came for a visit, but we are leaving now" he said.
"TJ" shouted a voice from the middle of the Farlights, "TJ" the voice shouted again.
TJ looked across the Farlights, he could not see who the voice belonged to and then suddenly, he spotted him. There in the middle of the Farlights was his best friend Linus. "Linus" he shouted as he ran across the cavern to him
"What are we doing here?" Linus asked.
"Have you forgotten" TJ asked, knowing that Linus wouldn't remember anything, "you fell over and banged your head on that rock, you must have got confused." He said.
"This place is impressive," said Linus.
"It sure is" said TJ, "Do you want to stay a little longer and have another look round?"
Linus looked around "Not much point in coming if I don't remember, so yea, let's go for another look and I'll be more careful this time." He laughed and TJ and Linus wandered off for another look around the cavern.
The other Farlights all looked very puzzled as none of them knew what they were doing there.

"Thank you for coming to visit the Cavern of Thunder" announced Inspector Sue, "we apologise for cutting your visit short" she said, "But we are going to have to end the tour now." She said. "If you make your way over here, we will escort you back to the surface."
One by one they got into the golden column with Berti and she ran her finger up the seam to take them back to the top of the mountain.
Gordon looked at Glinda, "we can go home now."
"But it's so beautiful in here" said Glinda, "can I take one last look round?" She asked
Gordon thought for a minute, what was a few more minutes, now he had Glinda back he was so happy. They could stay for an hour; they could even stay forever if he had Glinda by his side. Gordon took Glinda's hand "come on then" he said, "let's go look again."
As the Farlights were leaving, Inspector Sue wandered off around the cavern. By freeing everyone she had lost her Star. For so long she had kept the star safe and granted the dreams of those that needed them. She was not sure what she was going to do now.
She had been thinking so much, she had not realised, that she had wandered onto the bridge in the middle of the stream, in the middle of the cavern, in the middle of mountain. She gazed down into the stream. The water was gently running over the rocks and she smiled as she thought of all the people that she helped. She

hoped that she could help more, she just did not know if she could do it without the Star of KiKo. How would she get into the SS FATE without it?

"What are you thinking?" came a voice from behind her. Inspector Sue turned to find Victor and Vicky hovering at her side.

"What were you thinking about?" Asked Victor again.

"I was thinking about the Star of KiKo" she replied, "and all the people that I have granted dreams for"

"Have you checked your pocket?" Vicky asked

"Checked my pocket?" Said Inspector Sue looking puzzled, "What for?" She asked.

"Go ahead, check it" Vicky said

Inspector Sue put her hand over the pocket where she kept her Star and felt something there. She quickly put her hand in her pocket and pulled out her Star of KiKo.

"You are true of heart, you want to reward others, not yourself, your Star has come back to you" Vicky explained.

"I don't understand" said Inspector Sue, "all the Stars were inside the gold column, they all melted together."

"You are right" said Victor, "but the Stars know they need an owner for them to be able to do anything. The Stars knew that their owners had cared for them and that together they are more powerful than they are apart so once they had created the exit for you, all the Stars all returned

to their true owners.
Inspector Sue looked about the cavern. Gordon was walking around with Glinda; TJ was showing Linus around and the twins were sat on a rock chatting.
Inspector Sue turned back to Vicky and Victor, "does everyone have their star back?" she asked.
"If they are true of heart and either want or need it back, they will have it back" Vicky explained
"What about the seventh Star of KiKo?" Inspector Sue asked, "whose got that one?"
Vicky and Victor looked at each other, "that one has gone to someone very special" Vicky said, "someone that, even when faced with the hardest of challenges, has always thought of others before herself. Someone who has always looked after those around her and always done it with a smile on her face."
Inspector Sue looked around the cavern again trying to think of who it could be.
"Excuse me," said a young lady
Inspector Sue looked at her, she looked strangely familiar, but she did not know why.
"I think this must have fallen in my pocket whilst I was here," said the young lady.
She opened her hand and there lay the seventh Star of KiKo.
"What is your name?" Inspector Sue asked
"Shelly" the young lady replied
Inspector Sue suddenly realised that this was who Shelby was before she became a Farlight.

"Let's go sit over here, I have a story to tell you," said Inspector Sue. Shelly and Inspector Sue walked over to one of the rocks, sat down and Inspector Sue began to tell Shelly the story of the Star of KiKo.

Whilst Inspector Sue was telling the Shelly the story, one by one all the others found their stars in their pockets.

Gordon explained the story to Glinda and TJ explained it to Linus.

Once they had told their stories Glinda and Linus looked amazed. Had they really been trapped in here for so long? What was it like outside the mountain now? They had so many questions.

When Inspector Sue finished telling the story, Shelly was sad. Before she was taken by the dragon, she had always been bright and happy, or so everyone thought. In reality, she was not, she had no proper friends and all she wanted was to help people and be happy. It sounded like when she was a Farlight she was happy and she was helping people. "Do I have to be Shelly, could I go back to being Shelby?" She asked.

Inspector Sue thought for a minute, she did not see why not.

"I want to help people" Shelly said, "I want to stay here with TJ and help him, it sounds like I was happy here"

Shelly did not know, but Victor and Vicky had been floating nearby listening to the conversation. This was why they had given Shelly the seventh

Star. She was true of heart and only wanted to help others. So just like that they turned Shelly back into a Farlight and she became Shelby again.
Shelby was so happy; she flew about in big circles and then flew straight back to TJ's side.
"So, what do we do now?" Asked TJ
"Now," said Inspector Sue, "We make dreams come true."

Printed in Great Britain
by Amazon

87479226R00061